BIG and Little

Are Best Friends

To Katie.

Library of Congress Cataloging-in-Publication Data
Names: Garland, Michael, 1952— author, illustrator.
Title: Big and Little are best friends / Michael Garland.
Description: First edition. | New York : Orchard Books, an imprint of
Scholastic Inc., 2017. | © 2017 | Summary: Big is an elephant, and Little
is a mouse, and they like very different things, but despite their differences they remain the best of friends.
Identifiers: LCCN 2015049052 | ISBN 9780545870979 (hardcover : alk. paper)
Subjects: LCSH: Elephants—Juvenile fiction. | Mice—Juvenile fiction. | Best friends—Juvenile fiction.
| Difference (Psychology)—Juvenile fiction. | CYAC: Stories in rhyme. | Elephants—Fiction. | Mice—Fiction.
| Best friends—Fiction. | Friendship—Fiction. | Difference
(Psychology)—Fiction. | English language—Synonyms and antonyms—Fiction.
Classification: LCC PZ8.3.G185 Bi 2017 | DDC [E]—dc23 LC record available at http://lccn.loc.gov/2015049052

10 9 8 7 6 5 4 3 2 1   17 18 19 20 21

Printed in Malaysia   108
First edition, May 2017

The text and display text are set in KG blank Space Solid.
The artwork was sketched in pencil and painted digitally on a Wacom tablet in Photoshop.
Book design by Steve Ponzo

Visit Michael at www.garlandpicturebooks.com

BIG
and Little
Are Best Friends

Michael  Garland

Orchard Books • New York • An Imprint of Scholastic Inc.

Big and Little
Are best of friends,

Though the things
that they like
Are at opposite ends.

Big likes up,
Little likes down.

Little plays loud,
Big plays mellow.

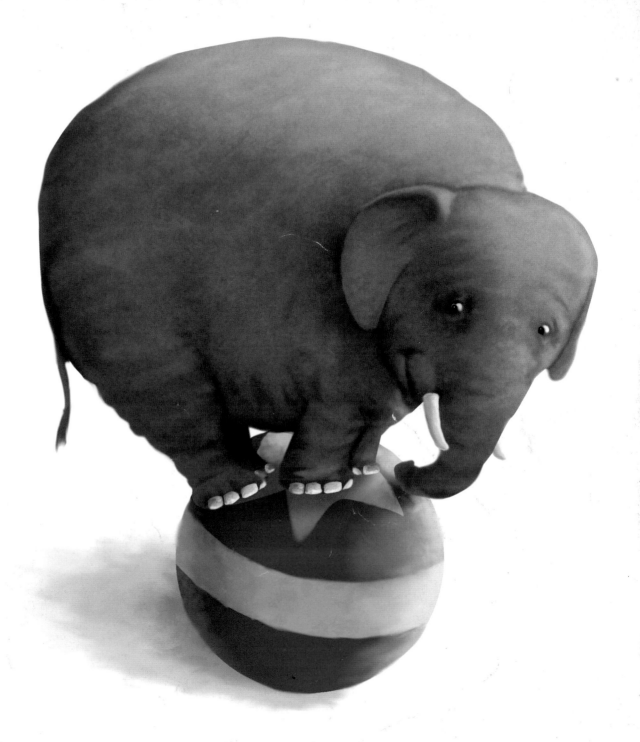

**Little likes square,
Big likes round.**

Little likes blue,
Big likes yellow.

Big takes naps,
While Little stays awake.

Big cooks spinach.

Little bakes cake.

Big loves hot,
Little loves cold.

Big is timid,
Little is bold.

Little likes to swim,
Big likes to row.

**Big goes fast,
Little goes slow.**

Little looks stern,
Big acts silly.

Big wears plain,
Little wears frilly.

Little's books are scary.
Big's books are sweet.

Because they are different
As day . . .

. . . and night,

These two best friends

Can sometimes fight.

But they always make up,

And it's always all right.

They may be different,
But don't think it strange.

They are who they are.
No need for a change!

Best friends can be opposites,
That's very true.

It works for Big and Little . . .

And for me and you.